Letters from the Earth

Earth

by Mark Twain

(1909)

This book has been published by:

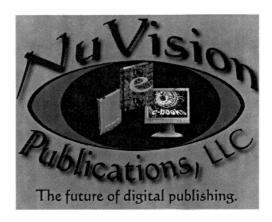

Contact: sales@nuvisionpublications.com

URL: http://www.nuvisionpublications.com

Publishing Date: 2008

ISBN# 1-59547-734-9

Please see our website for several books created for
education, research and entertainment.

Specializing in rare, out-of-print books still in demand.

NuVision Publications, LLC is dedicated to bringing new life to rare, historic, and formerly out-of-print books. Most re-print publishers simply photocopy, or scan and print the pages from the original book, which can make the book hard to read as most re-print books are 100+ years old. It is our policy to take the time to convert the original faded, sometimes blotched text into crisp, clear digital text. All of our printed books have been completely reformatted to be easy to read and enjoy.

Please note that we do not correct out-of-date facts or grammar-type errors that were in the original book. We do our best to retain the original composition of the text, the way the author intended it.

NuVision Publications, LLC
Sioux Falls, SD USA

Contents

The Creator sat upon the throne, thinking. Behind him stretched the illimitable continent of heaven, steeped in a glory of light and color; before him rose the black night of Space, like a wall. His mighty bulk towered rugged and mountain-like into the zenith, and His divine head blazed there like a distant sun. At His feet stood three colossal figures, diminished to extinction, almost, by contrast -- archangels -- their heads level with His ankle-bone.

When the Creator had finished thinking, He said, "I have thought. Behold!"

He lifted His hand, and from it burst a fountain-spray of fire, a million stupendous suns, which clove the blackness and soared, away and away and away, diminishing in magnitude and intensity as they pierced the far frontiers of Space, until at last they were but as diamond nailheads sparkling under the domed vast roof of the universe.

At the end of an hour the Grand Council was dismissed.

They left the Presence impressed and thoughtful, and retired to a private place, where they might talk with freedom. None of the three seemed to want to begin, though all wanted somebody to do it. Each was burning to discuss the great event, but would prefer not to commit himself till he should know how the others regarded it. So there was some aimless and halting conversation about matters of no consequence, and this dragged tediously along, arriving nowhere, until at last the archangel Satan gathered his courage together -- of which he had a very good supply -- and broke ground. He said: "We know what we are here to talk about, my lords, and we may as well put pretense aside, and begin. If this is the opinion of the Council -- "

"It is, it is!" said Gabriel and Michael, gratefully interrupting.

"Very well, then, let us proceed. We have witnessed a wonderful thing; as to that, we are necessarily agreed. As to the value of it -- if it has any -- that is a matter which does not personally concern us. We can have as many opinions about it as we like, and that is our limit. We have no vote. I think Space was well enough, just as it was, and useful, too. Cold and dark -- a restful place, now and then, after a season of the overdelicate climate and trying splendors of heaven. But these are details of no considerable moment; the new feature, the immense feature, is -- what, gentlemen?"

"The invention and introduction of automatic, unsupervised, self-regulating *law* for the government of those myriads of whirling and racing suns and worlds!"

"That is it!" said Satan. "You perceive that it is a stupendous idea. Nothing approaching it has been evolved from the Master Intellect before. Law -- *Automatic* Law -- exact and unvarying Law -- requiring

9

no watching, no correcting, no readjusting while the eternities endure! He said those countless vast bodies would plunge through the wastes of Space ages and ages, at unimaginable speed, around stupendous orbits, yet never collide, and never lengthen nor shorten their orbital periods by so much as the hundredth part of a second in two thousand years! That is the new miracle, and the greatest of all -- *Automatic Law!* And He gave it a name -- the LAW OF NATURE -- and said Natural Law is the LAW OF GOD -- interchangeable names for one and the same thing."

"Yes," said Michael, "and He said He would establish Natural Law -- the Law of God -- throughout His dominions, and its authority should be supreme and inviolable."

"Also," said Gabriel, "He said He would by and by create animals, and place them, likewise, under the authority of that Law."

"Yes," said Satan, "I heard Him, but did not understand. What *is* animals, Gabriel?"

"Ah, how should I know? How should any of us know? It is a new word."

[Interval of three centuries, celestial time -- the equivalent of a hundred million years, earthly time. Enter a Messenger-Angel.]

"My lords, He is making animals. Will it please you to come and see?"

They went, they saw, and were perplexed. Deeply perplexed -- and the Creator noticed it, and said, "Ask. I will answer."

"Divine One," said Satan, making obeisance, "what are they for?"

"They are an experiment in Morals and Conduct. Observe them, and be instructed."

There were thousands of them. They were full of activities. Busy, all busy -- mainly in persecuting each other. Satan remarked -- after examining one of them through a powerful microscope: "This large beast is killing weaker animals, Divine One."

"The tiger -- yes. The law of his nature is ferocity. The law of his nature is the Law of God. He cannot disobey it."

"Then in obeying it he commits no offense, Divine One?"

"No, he is blameless."

"This other creature, here, is timid, Divine One, and suffers death without resisting."

"The rabbit -- yes. He is without courage. It is the law of his nature -- the Law of God. He must obey it."

"Then he cannot honorably be required to go counter to his nature and resist, Divine One?"

"No. No creature can be honorably required to go counter to the law of his nature -- the Law of God."

After a long time and many questions, Satan said, "The spider kills the fly, and eats it; the bird kills the spider and eats it; the wildcat kills the goose; the -- well, they all kill each other. It is murder all along the line. Here are countless multitudes of creatures, and they all kill, kill, kill, they are all murderers. And they are not to blame, Divine One?"

"They are not to blame. It is the law of their nature. And always the law of nature is the Law of God. Now -- observe -- behold! A new creature -- and the masterpiece -- *Man!*"

Men, women, children, they came swarming in flocks, in droves, in millions.

"What shall you do with them, Divine One?"

"Put into each individual, in differing shades and degrees, all the various Moral Qualities, in mass, that have been distributed, a single distinguishing characteristic at a time, among the nonspeaking animal world -- courage, cowardice, ferocity, gentleness, fairness, justice, cunning, treachery, magnanimity, cruelty, malice, malignity, lust, mercy, pity, purity, selfishness, sweetness, honor, love, hate, baseness, nobility, loyalty, falsity, veracity, untruthfulness -- each human being shall have *all* of these in him, and they will constitute his nature. In some, there will be high and fine characteristics which will submerge the evil ones, and those will be called good men; in others the evil characteristics will have dominion, and those will be called bad men. Observe -- behold -- they vanish!"

"Whither are they gone, Divine One?"

"To the earth -- they and all their fellow animals."

"What is the earth?"

"A small globe I made, a time, two times and a half ago. You saw it, but did not notice it in the explosion of worlds and suns that sprayed from my hand. Man is an experiment, the other animals are another experiment. Time will show whether they were worth the trouble. The exhibition is over; you may take your leave, my lords."

Several days passed by.

11

This stands for a long stretch of (our) time, since in heaven a day is as a thousand years.

Satan had been making admiring remarks about certain of the Creator's sparkling industries -- remarks which, being read between the lines, were sarcasms. He had made them confidentially to his safe friends the other archangels, but they had been overheard by some ordinary angels and reported at Headquarters.

He was ordered into banishment for a day -- the celestial day. It was a punishment he was used to, on account of his too flexible tongue. Formerly he had been deported into Space, there being nowhither else to send him, and had flapped tediously around there in the eternal night and the Arctic chill; but now it occurred to him to push on and hunt up the earth and see how the Human-Race experiment was coming along.

By and by he wrote home -- very privately -- to St. Michael and St. Gabriel about it.

Satan's Letter

This is a strange place, and extraordinary place, and interesting. There is nothing resembling it at home. The people are all insane, the other animals are all insane, the earth is insane, Nature itself is insane. Man is a marvelous curiosity. When he is at his very very best he is a sort of low grade nickel-plated angel; at is worst he is unspeakable, unimaginable; and first and last and all the time he is a sarcasm. Yet he blandly and in all sincerity calls himself the "noblest work of God." This is the truth I am telling you. And this is not a new idea with him, he has talked it through all the ages, and believed it. Believed it, and found nobody among all his race to laugh at it.

Moreover -- if I may put another strain upon you -- he thinks he is the Creator's pet. He believes the Creator is proud of him; he even believes the Creator loves him; has a passion for him; sits up nights to admire him; yes, and watch over him and keep him out of trouble. He prays to Him, and thinks He listens. Isn't it a quaint idea? Fills his prayers with crude and bald and florid flatteries of Him, and thinks He sits and purrs over these extravagancies and enjoys them. He prays for help, and favor, and protection, every day; and does it with hopefulness and confidence, too, although no prayer of his has ever been answered. The daily affront, the daily defeat, do not discourage him, he goes on praying just the same. There is something almost fine about this perseverance. I must put one more strain upon you: he thinks he is going to heaven!

He has salaried teachers who tell him that. They also tell him there is a hell, of everlasting fire, and that he will go to it if he doesn't keep the Commandments. What are Commandments? They are a curiosity. I will tell you about them by and by.

Letter II

"I have told you nothing about man that is not true." You must pardon me if I repeat that remark now and then in these letters; I want you to take seriously the things I am telling you, and I feel that if I were in your place and you in mine, I should need that reminder from time to time, to keep my credulity from flagging.

For there is nothing about man that is not strange to an immortal. He looks at nothing as we look at it, his sense of proportion is quite different from ours, and his sense of values is so widely divergent from ours, that with all our large intellectual powers it is not likely that even the most gifted among us would ever be quite able to understand it.

For instance, take this sample: he has imagined a heaven, and has left entirely out of it the supremest of all his delights, the one ecstasy that stands first and foremost in the heart of every individual of his race -- and of ours -- sexual intercourse!

It is as if a lost and perishing person in a roasting desert should be told by a rescuer he might choose and have all longed-for things but one, and he should elect to leave out water!

His heaven is like himself: strange, interesting, astonishing, grotesque. I give you my word, it has not a single feature in it that he *actually values.* It consists -- utterly and entirely -- of diversions which he cares next to nothing about, here in the earth, yet is quite sure he will like them in heaven. Isn't it curious? Isn't it interesting? You must not think I am exaggerating, for it is not so. I will give you details.

Most men do not sing, most men cannot sing, most men will not stay when others are singing if it be continued more than two hours. Note that.

Only about two men in a hundred can play upon a musical instrument, and not four in a hundred have any wish to learn how. Set that down.

Many men pray, not many of them like to do it. A few pray long, the others make a short cut.

More men go to church than want to.

To forty-nine men in fifty the Sabbath Day is a dreary, dreary bore.

15

Of all the men in a church on a Sunday, two-thirds are tired when the service is half over, and the rest before it is finished.

The gladdest moment for all of them is when the preacher uplifts his hands for the benediction. You can hear the soft rustle of relief that sweeps the house, and you recognize that it is eloquent with gratitude.

All nations look down upon all other nations.

All nations dislike all other nations.

All white nations despise all colored nations, of whatever hue, and oppress them when they can.

White men will not associate with "niggers," nor marry them.

They will not allow them in their schools and churches.

All the world hates the Jew, and will not endure him except when he is rich.

I ask you to note all those particulars.

Further. All sane people detest noise.

All people, sane or insane, like to have variety in their life. Monotony quickly wearies them.

Every man, according to the mental equipment that has fallen to his share, exercises his intellect constantly, ceaselessly, and this exercise makes up a vast and valued and essential part of his life. The lowest intellect, like the highest, possesses a skill of some kind and takes a keen pleasure in testing it, proving it, perfecting it. The urchin who is his comrade's superior in games is as diligent and as enthusiastic in his practice as are the sculptor, the painter, the pianist, the mathematician and the rest. Not one of them could be happy if his talent were put under an interdict.

Now then, you have the facts. You know what the human race enjoys, and what it doesn't enjoy. It has invented a heaven out of its own head, all by itself: guess what it is like! In fifteen hundred eternities you couldn't do it. The ablest mind known to you or me in fifty million aeons couldn't do it. Very well, I will tell you about it.

1. First of all, I recall to your attention the extraordinary fact with which I began. To wit, that the human being, like the immortals, naturally places sexual intercourse far and away above all other joys -- yet he has left it out of his heaven! The very thought of it excites him; opportunity sets him wild; in this state he will risk life, reputation, everything -- even his queer heaven itself -- to make good that

16

opportunity and ride it to the overwhelming climax. From youth to middle age all men and all women prize copulation above all other pleasures combined, yet it is actually as I have said: it is not in their heaven; prayer takes its place.

They prize it thus highly; yet, like all their so-called "boons," it is a poor thing. At its very best and longest the act is brief beyond imagination -- the imagination of an immortal, I mean. In the matter of repetition the man is limited -- oh, quite beyond immortal conception. We who continue the act and its supremest ecstasies unbroken and without withdrawal for centuries, will never be able to understand or adequately pity the awful poverty of these people in that rich gift which, possessed as we possess it, makes all other possessions trivial and not worth the trouble of invoicing.

2. In man's heaven *everybody sings!* The man who did not sing on earth sings there; the man who could not sing on earth is able to do it there. The universal singing is not casual, not occasional, not relieved by intervals of quiet; it goes on, all day long, and every day, during a stretch of twelve hours. And *everybody stays;* whereas in the earth the place would be empty in two hours. The singing is of hymns alone. Nay, it is of *one* hymn alone. The words are always the same, in number they are only about a dozen, there is no rhyme, there is no poetry: "Hosannah, hosannah, hosannah, Lord God of Sabaoth, 'rah! 'rah! 'rah! siss! -- boom! ... a-a-ah!"

3. Meantime, every person is playing on a harp -- those millions and millions! -- whereas not more than twenty in the thousand of them could play an instrument in the earth, or ever wanted to.

Consider the deafening hurricane of sound -- millions and millions of voices screaming at once and millions and millions of harps gritting their teeth at the same time! I ask you: is it hideous, is it odious, is it horrible?

Consider further: it is a *praise* service; a service of compliment, of flattery, of adulation! Do you ask who it is that is willing to endure this strange compliment, this insane compliment; and who not only endures it, but likes it, enjoys it, requires if, *commands* it? Hold your breath!

It is God! This race's god, I mean. He sits on his throne, attended by his four and twenty elders and some other dignitaries pertaining to his court, and looks out over his miles and miles of tempestuous worshipers, and smiles, and purrs, and nods his satisfaction northward, eastward, southward; as quaint and nave a spectacle as has yet been imagined in this universe, I take it.

It is easy to see that the inventor of the heavens did not originate the idea, but copied it from the show-ceremonies of some sorry little sovereign State up in the back settlements of the Orient somewhere.

All sane white people hate noise; yet they have tranquilly accepted this kind of heaven -- without thinking, without reflection, without examination -- and they actually want to go to it! Profoundly devout old gray-headed men put in a large part of their time dreaming of the happy day when they will lay down the cares of this life and enter into the joys of that place. Yet you can see how unreal it is to them, and how little it takes a grip upon them as being fact, for they make no practical preparation for the great change: you never see one of them with a harp, you never hear one of them sing.

As you have seen, that singular show is a service of praise: praise by hymn, praise by prostration. It takes the place of "church." Now then, in the earth these people cannot stand much church -- an hour and a quarter is the limit, and they draw the line at once a week. That is to say, Sunday. One day in seven; and even then they do not look forward to it with longing. And so -- consider what their heaven provides for them: "church" that lasts forever, and a Sabbath that has no end! They quickly weary of this brief hebdomadal Sabbath here, yet they long for that eternal one; they dream of it, they talk about it, they *think* they think they are going to enjoy it -- with all their simple hearts they think they think they are going to be happy in it!

It is because they do not think at all; they only think they think. Whereas they can't think; not two human beings in ten thousand have anything to think with. And as to imagination -- oh, well, look at their heaven! They accept it, they approve it, they admire it. That gives you their intellectual measure.

4. The inventor of their heaven empties into it all the nations of the earth, in one common jumble. All are on an equality absolute, no one of them ranking another; they have to be "brothers"; they have to mix together, pray together, harp together, hosannah together -- whites, niggers, Jews, everybody -- there's no distinction. Here in the earth all nations hate each other, and every one of them hates the Jew. Yet every pious person adores that heaven and wants to get into it. He really does. And when he is in a holy rapture he thinks he thinks that if he were only there he would take all the populace to his heart, and hug, and hug, and hug!

He is a marvel -- man is! I would I knew who invented him.

5. Every man in the earth possesses some share of intellect, large or small; and be it large or be it small he takes pride in it. Also his heart swells at mention of the names of the majestic intellectual chiefs of his race, and he loves the tale of their splendid achievements. For he is of their blood, and in honoring themselves they have honored him. Lo, what the mind of man can do! he cries, and calls the roll of the illustrious of all ages; and points to the imperishable literatures they have given to the world, and the mechanical wonders they have

invented, and the glories wherewith they have clothed science and the arts; and to them he uncovers as to kings, and gives to them the profoundest homage, and the sincerest, his exultant heart can furnish -- thus exalting intellect above all things else in the world, and enthroning it there under the arching skies in a supremacy unapproachable. And then he contrived a heaven that hasn't a rag of intellectuality in it anywhere!

Is it odd, is it curious, is it puzzling? It is exactly as I have said, incredible as it may sound. This sincere adorer of intellect and prodigal rewarder of its mighty services here in the earth has invented a religion and a heaven which pay no compliments to intellect, offer it no distinctions, fling it no largess: in fact, never even mention it.

By this time you will have noticed that the human being's heaven has been thought out and constructed upon an absolute definite plan; and that this plan is, that it shall contain, in labored detail, each and every imaginable thing that is repulsive to a man, and not a single thing he likes!

Very well, the further we proceed the more will this curious fact be apparent.

Make a note of it: in man's heaven there are no exercises for the intellect, nothing for it to live upon. It would rot there in a year -- rot and stink. Rot and stink -- and at that stage become holy. A blessed thing: for only the holy can stand the joys of that bedlam.

Letter III

You have noticed that the human being is a curiosity. In times past he has had (and worn out and flung away) hundreds and hundreds of religions; today he has hundreds and hundreds of religions, and launches not fewer than three new ones every year. I could enlarge that number and still be within the facts.

One of his principle religions is called the Christian. A sketch of it will interest you. It sets forth in detail in a book containing two million words, called the Old and New Testaments. Also it has another name -- The Word of God. For the Christian thinks every word of it was dictated by God -- the one I have been speaking of.

It is full of interest. It has noble poetry in it; and some clever fables; and some blood-drenched history; and some good morals; and a wealth of obscenity; and upwards of a thousand lies.

This Bible is built mainly out of the fragments of older Bibles that had their day and crumbled to ruin. So it noticeably lacks in originality, necessarily. Its three or four most imposing and impressive events all happened in earlier Bibles; all its best precepts and rules of conduct came also from those Bibles; there are only two new things in it: hell, for one, and that singular heaven I have told you about.

What shall we do? If we believe, with these people, that their God invented these cruel things, we slander him; if we believe that these people invented them themselves, we slander them. It is an unpleasant dilemma in either case, for neither of these parties has done us any harm.

For the sake of tranquility, let us take a side. Let us join forces with the people and put the whole ungracious burden upon *him* -- heaven, hell, Bible and all. It does not seem right, it does not seem fair; and yet when you consider that heaven, and how crushingly charged it is with everything that is repulsive to a human being, how can we believe a human being invented it? And when I come to tell you about hell, the stain will be greater still, and you will be likely to say, No, a man would not provide that place, for either himself or anybody else; he simply couldn't.

That innocent Bible tells about the Creation. Of what -- the universe? Yes, the universe. In six days!

God did it. He did not call it the universe -- that name is modern. His whole attention was upon this world. He constructed it in five days -- and then? It took him only one day to make twenty million suns and eighty million planets!

What were they for -- according to this idea? To furnish light for this little toy-world. That was his whole purpose; he had no other. One of the twenty million suns (the smallest one) was to light it in the daytime, the rest were to help one of the universe's countless moons modify the darkness of its nights.

It is quite manifest that he believed his fresh-made skies were diamond-sown with those myriads of twinkling stars the moment his first-day's sun sank below the horizon; whereas, in fact, not a single star winked in that black vault until three years and a half after that memorable week's formidable industries had been completed.[1] Then one star appeared, all solitary and alone, and began to blink. Three years later another one appeared. The two blinked together for more than four years before a third joined them. At the end of the first hundred years there were not yet twenty-five stars twinkling in the wide wastes of those gloomy skies. At the end of a thousand years not enough stars were yet visible to make a show. At the end of a million years only half of the present array had sent their light over the telescopic frontiers, and it took another million for the rest to follow suit, as the vulgar phrase goes. There being at that time no telescope, their advent was not observed.

For three hundred years, now, the Christian astronomer has known that his Deity didn't make the stars in those tremendous six days; but the Christian astronomer does not enlarge upon that detail. Neither does the priest.

In his Book, God is eloquent in his praises of his mighty works, and calls them by the largest names he can find -- thus indicating that he has a strong and just admiration of magnitudes; yet he made those millions of prodigious suns to light this wee little orb, instead of appointing this orb's little sun to dance attendance upon them. He mentions Arcturus in his book -- you remember Arcturus; we went there once. It is one of the earth's night lamps! -- that giant globe which is fifty thousand times as large as the earth's sun, and compares with it as a melon compares with a cathedral.

However, the Sunday school still teaches the child that Arcturus was created to help light this earth, and the child grows up and continues to

---

[1] It takes the light of the nearest star (61 Cygni) three and a half years to come to the earth, traveling at the rate of 186,000 miles per second. Arcturus had been shining 200 years before it was visible from the earth. Remoter stars gradually became visible after thousands and thousands of years. -- The Editor [M. T.]

believe it long after he has found out that the probabilities are against it being so.

According to the Book and its servants the universe is only six thousand years old. It is only within the last hundred years that studious, inquiring minds have found out that it is nearer a hundred million.

During the Six Days, God created man and the other animals.

He made a man and a woman and placed them in a pleasant garden, along with the other creatures. they all lived together there in harmony and contentment and blooming youth for some time; then trouble came. God had warned the man and the woman that they must not eat of the fruit of a certain tree. And he added a most strange remark: he said that if they ate of it they should surely die. Strange, for the reason that inasmuch as they had never seen a sample death they could not possibly know what he meant. Neither would he nor any other god have been able to make those ignorant children understand what was meant, without furnishing a sample. The mere word could have no meaning for them, any more than it would have for an infant of days.

Presently a serpent sought them out privately, and came to them walking upright, which was the way of serpents in those days. The serpent said the forbidden fruit would store their vacant minds with knowledge. So they ate it, which was quite natural, for man is so made that he eagerly wants to know; whereas the priest, like God, whose imitator and representative he is, has made it his business from the beginning to keep him from knowing any useful thing.

Adam and Eve ate the forbidden fruit, and at once a great light streamed into their dim heads. They had acquired knowledge. What knowledge -- useful knowledge? No -- merely knowledge that there was such a thing as good, and such a thing as evil, and how to do evil. they couldn't do it before. Therefore all their acts up to this time had been without stain, without blame, without offense.

But now they could do evil -- and suffer for it; now they had acquired what the Church calls an invaluable possession, the Moral Sense; that sense which differentiates man from the beast and sets him above the beast. Instead of below the beast -- where one would suppose his proper place would be, since he is always foul-minded and guilty and the beast always clean-minded and innocent. It is like valuing a watch that must go wrong, above a watch that can't.

The Church still prizes the Moral Sense as man's noblest asset today, although the Church knows God had a distinctly poor opinion of it and did what he could in his clumsy way to keep his happy Children of the Garden from acquiring it.

23

Very well, Adam and Eve now knew what evil was, and how to do it. They knew how to do various kinds of wrong things, and among them one principal one -- the one God had his mind on principally. That one was the art and mystery of sexual intercourse. To them it was a magnificent discovery, and they stopped idling around and turned their entire attention to it, poor exultant young things!

In the midst of one of these celebrations they heard God walking among the bushes, which was an afternoon custom of his, and they were smitten with fright. Why? Because they were naked. They had not known it before. They had not minded it before; neither had God.

In that memorable moment immodesty was born; and some people have valued it ever since, though it would certainly puzzle them to explain why.

Adam and Eve entered the world naked and unashamed -- naked and pure-minded; and no descendant of theirs has ever entered it otherwise. All have entered it naked, unashamed, and clean in mind. They have entered it modest. They had to acquire immodesty and the soiled mind; there was no other way to get it. A Christian mother's first duty is to soil her child's mind, and she does not neglect it. Her lad grows up to be a missionary, and goes to the innocent savage and to the civilized Japanese, and soils their minds. Whereupon they adopt immodesty, they conceal their bodies, they stop bathing naked together.

The convention miscalled modesty has no standard, and cannot have one, because it is opposed to nature and reason, and is therefore an artificiality and subject to anybody's whim, anybody's diseased caprice. And so, in India the refined lady covers her face and breasts and leaves her legs naked from the hips down, while the refined European lady covers her legs and exposes her face and her breasts. In lands inhabited by the innocent savage the refined European lady soon gets used to full-grown native stark-nakedness, and ceases to be offended by it. A highly cultivated French count and countess -- unrelated to each other -- who were marooned in their nightclothes, by shipwreck, upon an uninhabited island in the eighteenth century, were soon naked. Also ashamed -- for a week. After that their nakedness did not trouble them, and they soon ceased to think about it.

You have never seen a person with clothes on. Oh, well, you haven't lost anything.

To proceed with the Biblical curiosities. Naturally you will think the threat to punish Adam and Eve for disobeying was of course not carried out, since they did not create themselves, nor their natures nor their impulses nor their weaknesses, and hence were not properly subject to anyone's commands, and not responsible to anybody for their acts. It will surprise you to know that the threat was carried out. Adam and Eve

24

were punished, and that crime finds apologists unto this day. The sentence of death was executed.

As you perceive, the only person responsible for the couple's offense escaped; and not only escaped but became the executioner of the innocent.

In your country and mine we should have the privilege of making fun of this kind of morality, but it would be unkind to do it here. Many of these people have the reasoning faculty, but no one uses it in religious matters.

The best minds will tell you that when a man has begotten a child he is morally bound to tenderly care for it, protect it from hurt, shield it from disease, clothe it, feed it, bear with its waywardness, lay no hand upon it save in kindness and for its own good, and never in any case inflict upon it a wanton cruelty. God's treatment of his earthly children, every day and every night, is the exact opposite of all that, yet those best minds warmly justify these crimes, condone them, excuse them, and indignantly refuse to regard them as crimes at all, when *he* commits them. Your country and mine is an interesting one, but there is nothing there that is half so interesting as the human mind.

Very well, God banished Adam and Eve from the Garden, and eventually assassinated them. All for disobeying a command which he had no right to utter. But he did not stop there, as you will see. He has one code of morals for himself, and quite another for his children. He requires his children to deal justly -- and gently -- with offenders, and forgive them seventy-and-seven times; whereas he deals neither justly nor gently with anyone, and he did not forgive the ignorant and thoughtless first pair of juveniles even their first small offense and say, "You may go free this time, and I will give you another chance."

On the contrary! He elected to punish *their* children, all through the ages to the end of time, for a trifling offense committed by others before they were born. He is punishing them yet. In mild ways? No, in atrocious ones.

You would not suppose that this kind of Being gets many compliments. Undeceive yourself: the world calls him the All-Just, the All-Righteous, the All-Good, the All-Merciful, the All-Forgiving, the All-Truthful, the All-Loving, the Source of All Morality. These sarcasms are uttered daily, all over the world. But not as conscious sarcasms. No, they are meant seriously: they are uttered without a smile.

Letter IV

So the First Pair went forth from the Garden under a curse -- a permanent one. They had lost every pleasure they had possessed before "The Fall"; and yet they were rich, for they had gained one worth all the rest: they knew the Supreme Art.

They practiced it diligently and were filled with contentment. The Deity ordered them to practice it. They obeyed, this time. But it was just as well it was not forbidden, for they would have practiced it anyhow, if a thousand Deities had forbidden it.

Results followed. By the name of Cain and Abel. And these had some sisters; and knew what to do with them. And so there were some more results: Cain and Abel begot some nephews and nieces. These, in their turn, begot some second cousins. At this point classification of relationships began to get difficult, and the attempt to keep it up was abandoned.

The pleasant labor of populating the world went on from age to age, and with prime efficiency; for in those happy days the sexes were still competent for the Supreme Art when by rights they ought to have been dead eight hundred years. The sweeter sex, the dearer sex, the lovelier sex was manifestly at its very best, then, for it was even able to attract gods. Real gods. They came down out of heaven and had wonderful times with those hot young blossoms. The Bible tells about it.

By help of those visiting foreigners the population grew and grew until it numbered several millions. But it was a disappointment to the Deity. He was dissatisfied with its morals; which in some respects were not any better than his own. Indeed they were an unflatteringly close imitation of his own. They were a very bad people, and as he knew of no way to reform them, he wisely concluded to abolish them. This is the only really enlightened and superior idea his Bible has credited him with, and it would have made his reputation for all time if he could only have kept to it and carried it out. But he was always unstable -- except in his advertisements -- and his good resolution broke down. He took a pride in man; man was his finest invention; man was his pet, after the housefly, and he could not bear to lose him wholly; so he finally decided to save a sample of him and drown the rest.

Nothing could be more characteristic of him. He created all those infamous people, and he alone was responsible for their conduct. Not one of them deserved death, yet it was certainly good policy to extinguish them; especially since in creating them the master crime had already been committed, and to allow them to go on procreating would be a distinct addition to the crime. But at the same time there could be no justice, no fairness, in any favoritism -- all should be drowned or none.

No, he would not have it so; he would save half a dozen and try the race over again. He was not able to foresee that it would go rotten again, for he is only the Far-Sighted One in his advertisements.

He saved out Noah and his family, and arranged to exterminate the rest. He planned an Ark, and Noah built it. Neither of them had ever built an Ark before, nor knew anything about Arks; and so something out of the common was to be expected. It happened. Noah was a farmer, and although he knew what was required of the Ark he was quite incompetent to say whether this one would be large enough to meet the requirements or not (which it wasn't), so he ventured no advice. The Deity did not know it wasn't large enough, but took the chances and made no adequate measurements. In the end the ship fell far short of the necessities, and to this day the world still suffers for it.

Noah built the Ark. He built it the best he could, but left out most of the essentials. It had no rudder, it had no sails, it had no compass, it had no pumps, it had no charts, no lead-lines, no anchors, no log, no light, no ventilation, and as for cargo room -- which was the main thing -- the less said about that the better. It was to be at sea eleven months, and would need fresh water enough to fill two Arks of its size -- yet the additional Ark was not provided. Water from outside could not be utilized: half of it would be salt water, and men and land animals could not drink it.

For not only was a sample of man to be saved, but business samples of the other animals, too. You must understand that when Adam ate the apple in the Garden and learned how to multiply and replenish, the other animals learned the Art, too, by watching Adam. It was cunning of them, it was neat; for they got all that was worth having out of the apple without tasting it and afflicting themselves with the disastrous Moral Sense, the parent of all immoralities.

Letter V

Noah began to collect animals. There was to be one couple of each and every sort of creature that walked or crawled, or swam or flew, in the world of animated nature. We have to guess at how long it took to collect the creatures and how much it cost, for there is no record of these details. When Symmachus made preparation to introduce his young son to grown-up life in imperial Rome, he sent men to Asia, Africa and everywhere to collect wild animals for the arena-fights. It took the men three years to accumulate the animals and fetch them to Rome. Merely quadrupeds and alligators, you understand -- no birds, no snakes, no frogs, no worms, no lice, no rats, no fleas, no ticks, no caterpillars, no spiders, no houseflies, no mosquitoes -- nothing but just plain simple quadrupeds and alligators: and no quadrupeds except fighting ones. Yet it was as I have said: it took three years to collect them, and the cost of animals and transportation and the men's wages footed up $4,500,000.

How many animals? We do not know. But it was under five thousand, for that was the largest number ever gathered for those Roman shows, and it was Titus, not Symmachus, who made that collection. Those were mere baby museums, compared to Noah's contract. Of birds and beasts and fresh-water creatures he had to collect 146,000 kinds; and of insects upwards of two million species.

Thousands and thousands of those things are very difficult to catch, and if Noah had not given up and resigned, he would be on the job yet, as Leviticus used to say. However, I do not mean that he withdrew. No, he did not do that. He gathered as many creatures as he had room for, and then stopped.

If he had known all the requirements in the beginning, he would have been aware that what was needed was a fleet of Arks. But he did not know how many kinds of creatures there were, neither did his Chief. So he had no Kangaroo, and no 'possom, and no Gila monster, and no ornithorhynchus, and lacked a multitude of other indispensable blessings which a loving Creator had provided for man and forgotten about, they having long ago wandered to a side of this world which he had never seen and with whose affairs he was not acquainted. And so everyone of them came within a hair of getting drowned.

They only escaped by an accident. There was not water enough to go around. Only enough was provided to flood one small corner of the globe -- the rest of the globe was not then known, and was supposed to be nonexistent.

However, the thing that really and finally and definitely determined Noah to stop with enough species for purely business purposes and let the rest become extinct, was an incident of the last days: an excited stranger arrived with some most alarming news. He said he had been camping among some mountains and valleys about six hundred miles away, and he had seen a wonderful thing there: he stood upon a precipice overlooking a wide valley, and up the valley he was a billowy black sea of strange animal life coming. Presently the creatures passed by, struggling, fighting, scrambling, screeching, snorting -- horrible vast masses of tumultuous flesh! Sloths as big as an elephant; frogs as big as a cow; a megatherium and his harem huge beyond belief; saurians and saurians and saurians, group after group, family after family, species after species -- a hundred feet long, thirty feet high, and twice as quarrelsome; one of them hit a perfectly blameless Durham bull a thump with its tail and sent it whizzing three hundred feet into the air and it fell at the man's feet with a sigh and was no more. The man said that these prodigious animals had heard about the Ark and were coming. Coming to get saved from the flood. And not coming in pairs, they were *all* coming: they did not know the passengers were restricted to pairs, the man said, and wouldn't care a rap for the regulations, anyway -- they would sail in that Ark or know the reason why. The man said the Ark would not hold the half of them; and moreover they were coming hungry, and would eat up everything there was, including the menagerie and the family.

All these facts were suppressed, in the Biblical account. You find not a hint of them there. The whole thing is hushed up. Not even the names of those vast creatures are mentioned. It shows you that when people have left a reproachful vacancy in a contract they can be as shady about it in Bibles as elsewhere. Those powerful animals would be of inestimable value to man now, when transportation is so hard pressed and expensive, but they are all lost to him. All lost, and by Noah's fault. They all got drowned. Some of them as much as eight million years ago.

Very well, the stranger told his tale, and Noah saw that he must get away before the monsters arrived. He would have sailed at once, but the upholsterers and decorators of the housefly's drawing room still had some finishing touches to put on, and that lost him a day. Another day was lost in getting the flies aboard, there being sixty-eight billions of them and the Deity still afraid there might not be enough. Another day was lost in stowing forty tons of selected filth for the flies' sustenance.

Then at last, Noah sailed; and none too soon, for the Ark was only just sinking out of sight on the horizon when the monsters arrived, and added their lamentations to those of the multitude of weeping fathers and mothers and frightened little children who were clinging to the wave-washed rocks in the pouring rain and lifting imploring prayers to an All-Just and All-Forgiving and All-Pitying Being who had never answered a prayer since those crags were builded, grain by grain, out of the sands, and would still not have answered one when the ages should have crumbled them to sand again.

Letter VI

On the third day, about noon, it was found that a fly and been left behind. The return voyage turned out to be long and difficult, on account of the lack of chart and compass, and because of the changed aspects of all coasts, the steadily rising water having submerged some of the lower landmarks and given to higher ones an unfamiliar look; but after sixteen days of earnest and faithful seeking, the fly was found at last, and received on board with hymns of praise and gratitude, the Family standing meanwhile uncovered, our of reverence for its divine origin. It was weary and worn, and had suffered somewhat from the weather, but was otherwise in good estate. Men and their families had died of hunger on barren mountain tops, but it had not lacked for food, the multitudinous corpses furnishing it in rank and rotten richness. Thus was the sacred bird providentially preserved.

Providentially. That is the word. For the fly had not been left behind by accident. No, the hand of Providence was in it. There are no accidents. All things that happen, happen for a purpose. They are foreseen from the beginning of time, they are ordained from the beginning of time. From the dawn of Creation the Lord had foreseen that Noah, being alarmed and confused by the invasion of the prodigious brevet fossils, would prematurely fly to sea unprovided with a certain invaluable disease. He would have all the other diseases, and could distribute them among the new races of men as they appeared in the world, but he would lack one of the very best -- typhoid fever; a malady which, when the circumstances are especially favorable, is able to utterly wreck a patient without killing him; for it can restore him to his feet with a long life in him, and yet deaf, dumb, blind, crippled, and idiotic. The housefly is its main disseminator, and is more competent and more calamitously effective than all the other distributors of the dreaded scourge put together. And so, by foreordination from the beginning of time, this fly was left behind to seek out a typhoid corpse and feed upon its corruptions and gaum its legs with germs and transmit them to the re-peopled world for permanent business. From that one housefly, in the ages that have since elapsed, billions of sickbeds have been stocked, billions of wrecked bodies sent tottering about the earth, and billions of cemeteries recruited with the dead.

It is most difficult to understand the disposition of the Bible God, it is such a confusion of contradictions; of watery instabilities and iron firmness; of goody-goody abstract morals made out of words, and concreted hell-born ones made out of acts; of fleeting kindness repented of in permanent malignities.

33

However, when after much puzzling you get at the key to his disposition, you do at last arrive at a sort of understanding of it. With a most quaint and juvenile and astonishing frankness he has furnished that key himself. It is jealousy!

I expect that to take your breath away. You are aware -- for I have already told you in an earlier letter -- that among human beings jealousy ranks distinctly as a weakness; a trade-mark of small minds; a property of *all* small minds, yet a property which even the smallest is ashamed of; and when accused of its possession will lyingly deny it and resent the accusation as an insult.

Jealousy. Do not forget it, keep it in mind. It is the key. With it you will come to partly understand God as we go along; without it nobody can understand him. As I have said, he has openly held up this treasonous key himself, for all to see. He says, naïvely, outspokenly, and without suggestion of embarrassment: "I the Lord thy God am a jealous God."

You see, it is only another way of saying, "I the Lord thy God am a small God; a small God, and fretful about small things."

He was giving a warning: he could not bear the thought of any other God getting some of the Sunday compliments of this comical little human race -- he wanted all of them for himself. He valued them. To him they were riches; just as tin money is to a Zulu.

But wait -- I am not fair; I am misrepresenting him; prejudice is beguiling me into saying what is not true. He did not say he wanted all of the adulations; he said nothing about not being willing to share them with his fellow gods; what he said was, "Thou shalt have no other gods *before* me."

It is a quite different thing, and puts him in a much better light -- I confess it. There was an abundance of gods, the woods were full of them, as the saying is, and all he demanded was that he should be ranked as high as the others -- not above any of them, but not below any of them. He was willing that they should fertilize earthly virgins, but not on any better terms than he could have for himself in his turn. He wanted to be held their equal. This he insisted upon, in the clearest language: he would have no other gods *before* him. They could march abreast with him, but none of them could head the procession, and he did not claim the right to head it himself.

Do you think he was able to stick to that upright and creditable position? No. He could keep to a bad resolution forever, but he couldn't keep to a good one a month. By and by he threw aside and calmly claimed to be the only God in the entire universe.

As I was saying, jealousy is the key; all through his history it is present and prominent. It is the blood and bone of his disposition, it is the basis of his character. How small a thing can wreck his composure and disorder his judgement if it touches the raw of his jealousy! And nothing warms up this trait so quickly and so surely and so exaggeratedly as a suspicion that some competition with the god-Trust is impending. The fear that if Adam and Eve ate of the fruit of the Tree of Knowledge they would "be as gods" so fired his jealousy that his reason was affected, and he could not treat those poor creatures either fairly or charitably, or even refrain from dealing cruelly and criminally with their blameless posterity.

To this day his reason has never recovered from that shock; a wild nightmare of vengefulness has possessed him ever since, and he has almost bankrupted his native ingenuities in inventing pains and miseries and humiliations and heartbreaks wherewith to embitter the brief lives of Adam's descendants. Think of the diseases he has contrived for them! They are multitudinous; no book can name them all. And each one is a trap, set for an innocent victim.

The human being is a machine. An automatic machine. It is composed of thousands of complex and delicate mechanisms, which perform their functions harmoniously and perfectly, in accordance with laws devised for their governance, and over which the man himself has no authority, no mastership, no control. For each one of these thousands of mechanisms the Creator has planned an enemy, whose office is to harass it, pester it, persecute it, damage it, afflict it with pains, and miseries, and ultimate destruction. Not one has been overlooked.

From cradle to grave these enemies are always at work; they know no rest, night or day. They are an army: an organized army; a besieging army; an assaulting army; an army that is alert, watchful, eager, merciless; an army that never relents, never grants a truce.

It moves by squad, by company, by battalion, by regiment, by brigade, by division, by army corps; upon occasion it masses its parts and moves upon mankind with its whole strength. It is the Creator's Grand Army, and he is the Commander-in-Chief. Along its battlefront its grisly banners wave their legends in the face of the sun: Disaster, Disease, and the rest.

Disease! That is the main force, the diligent force, the devastating force! It attacks the infant the moment it is born; it furnishes it one malady after another: croup, measles, mumps, bowel troubles, teething pains, scarlet fever, and other childhood specialties. It chases the child into youth and furnishes it some specialties for that time of life. It chases the youth into maturity, maturity into age, age into the grave.

With these facts before you will you now try to guess man's chiefest pet name for this ferocious Commander-in-Chief? I will save you the trouble -- but you must not laugh. It is Our Father in Heaven!

It is curious -- the way the human mind works. The Christian begins with this straight proposition, this definite proposition, this inflexible and uncompromising proposition: *God is all-knowing, and all-powerful.*

This being the case, nothing can happen without his knowing beforehand that it is going to happen; nothing happens without his permission; nothing can happen that he chooses to prevent.

That is definite enough, isn't it? It makes the Creator distinctly responsible for everything that happens, doesn't it?

The Christian concedes it in that italicized sentence. Concedes it with feeling, with enthusiasm.

Then, having thus made the Creator responsible for all those pains and diseases and miseries above enumerated, and which he could have prevented, the gifted Christian blandly calls him Our Father!

It is as I tell you. He equips the Creator with every trait that goes to the making of a fiend, and then arrives at the conclusion that a fiend and a father are the same thing! Yet he would deny that a malevolent lunatic and a Sunday school superintendent are essentially the same. What do you think of the human mind? I mean, in case you think there is a human mind.

Letter VII

Noah and his family were saved -- if that could be called an advantage. I throw in the *if* for the reason that there has never been an intelligent person of the age of sixty who would consent to live his life over again. His or anyone else's. The Family were saved, yes, but they were not comfortable, for they were full of microbes. Full to the eyebrows; fat with them, obese with them, distended like balloons. It was a disagreeable condition, but it could not be helped, because enough microbes had to be saved to supply the future races of men with desolating diseases, and there were but eight persons on board to serve as hotels for them. The microbes were by far the most important part of the Ark's cargo, and the part the Creator was most anxious about and most infatuated with. They had to have good nourishment and pleasant accommodations. There were typhoid germs, and cholera germs, and hydrophobia germs, and lockjaw germs, and consumption germs, and black-plague germs, and some hundreds of other aristocrats, specially precious creations, golden bearers of God's love to man, blessed gifts of the infatuated Father to his children -- all of which had to be sumptuously housed and richly entertained; these were located in the choicest places the interiors of the Family could furnish: in the lungs, in the heart, in the brain, in the kidneys, in the blood, in the guts. In the guts particularly. The great intestine was the favorite resort. There they gathered, by countless billions, and worked, and fed, and squirmed, and sang hymns of praise and thanksgiving; and at night when it was quiet you could hear the soft murmur of it. The large intestine was in effect their heaven. They stuffed it solid; they made it as rigid as a coil of gaspipe. They took pride in this. Their principal hymn made gratified reference to it:

Constipation, O Constipation,
The Joyful sound proclaim
Till man's remotest entrail
Shall praise its Maker's name

The discomforts furnished by the Ark were many and various. The family had to live right in the presence of the multitudinous animals, and breathe the distressing stench they make and be deafened day and night with the thunder-crash of noise their roarings and screechings produced; and in additions to these intolerable discomforts it was a peculiarly trying place for the ladies, for they could look in no direction without seeing some thousands of the creatures engaged in multiplying and replenishing. And then, there were the flies. They swarmed everywhere, and persecuted the Family all day long. They were the first

37

animals up, in the morning, and the last ones down, at night. But they must not be killed, they must not be injured, they were sacred, their origin was divine, they were the special pets of the Creator, his darlings.

By and by the other creatures would be distributed here and there about the earth -- scattered: the tigers to India, the lions and the elephants to the vacant desert and the secret places of the jungle, the birds to the boundless regions of empty space, the insects to one or another climate, according to nature and requirement; but the fly? He is of no nationality; all the climates are his home, all the globe is his province, all creatures that breathe are his prey, and unto them all he is a scourge and a hell.

To man he is a divine ambassador, a minister plenipotentiary, the Creator's special representative. He infests him in his cradle; clings in bunches to his gummy eyelids; buzzes and bites and harries him, robbing him of his sleep and his weary mother of her strength in those long vigils which she devotes to protecting her child from this pest's persecutions. The fly harries the sick man in his home, in the hospital, even on his deathbed at his last gasp. Pesters him at his meals; previously hunts up patients suffering from loathsome and deadly diseases; wades in their sores, gaums its legs with a million death-dealing germs; then comes to that healthy man's table and wipes these things off on the butter and discharges a bowel-load of typhoid germs and excrement on his batter-cakes. The housefly wrecks more human constitutions and destroys more human lives than all God's multitude of misery-messengers and death-agents put together.

Shem was full of hookworms. It is wonderful, the thorough and comprehensive study which the Creator devoted to the great work of making man miserable. I have said he devised a special affliction-agent for each and every detail of man's structure, overlooking not a single one, and I said the truth. Many poor people have to go barefoot, because they cannot afford shoes. The Creator saw his opportunity. I will remark, in passing, that he always has his eye on the poor. Nine-tenths of his disease-inventions were intended for the poor, and they get them. The well-to-do get only what is left over. Do not suspect me of speaking unheedfully, for it is not so: the vast bulk of the Creator's affliction-inventions are specially designed for the persecution of the poor. You could guess this by the fact that one of the pulpit's finest and commonest names for the Creator is "The Friend of the Poor." Under no circumstances does the pulpit ever pay the Creator a compliment that has a vestige of truth in it. The poor's most implacable and unwearying enemy is their Father in Heaven. The poor's only real friend is their fellow man. He is sorry for them, he pities them, and he shows it by his deeds. He does much to relieve their distresses; and in every case their Father in Heaven gets the credit of it.

Just so with diseases. If science exterminates a disease which has been working for God, it is God that gets the credit, and all the pulpits break into grateful advertising-raptures and call attention to how good he is! Yes, *he* has done it. Perhaps he has waited a thousand years before doing it. That is nothing; the pulpit says he was thinking about it all the time. When exasperated men rise up and sweep away an age-long tyranny and set a nation free, the first thing the delighted pulpit does is to advertise it as God's work, and invite the people to get down on their knees and pour out their thanks to him for it. And the pulpit says with admiring emotion, "Let tyrants understand that the Eye that never sleeps is upon them; and let them remember that the Lord our God will not always be patient, but will loose the whirlwinds of his wrath upon them in his appointed day."

They forget to mention that he is the slowest mover in the universe; that his Eye that never sleeps, might as well, since it takes it a century to see what any other eye would see in a week; that in all history there is not an instance where he thought of a noble deed *first*, but always thought of it just a little after somebody else had thought of it and *done* it. He arrives then, and annexes the dividend.

Very well, six thousand years ago Shem was full of hookworms. Microscopic in size, invisible to the unaided eye. All of the Creator's specially deadly disease-producers are invisible. It is an ingenious idea. For thousands of years it kept man from getting at the roots of his maladies, and defeated his attempts to master them. It is only very recently that science has succeeded in exposing some of these treacheries.

The very latest of these blessed triumphs of science is the discovery and identification of the ambuscaded assassin which goes by the name of the hookworm. Its special prey is the barefooted poor. It lies in wait in warm regions and sandy places and digs its way Into their unprotected feet.

The hookworm was discovered two or three years ago by a physician, who had been patiently studying its victims for a long time. The disease induced by the hookworm had been doing its evil work here and there in the earth ever since Shem landed on Ararat, but it was never suspected to *be* a disease at all. The people who had it were merely supposed to be *lazy*, and were therefore despised and made fun of, when they should have been pitied. The hookworm is a peculiarly sneaking and underhanded invention, and has done its surreptitious work unmolested for ages; but that physician and his helpers will exterminate it now.

God is back of this. He has been thinking about it for six thousand years, and making up his mind. The idea of exterminating the hookworm was his. He came very near doing it before Dr. Charles Wardell Stiles did. But he is in time to get the credit of it. He always is.

It is going to cost a million dollars. He was probably just in the act of contributing that sum when a man pushed in ahead of him -- as usual.

Mr. Rockefeller. He furnishes the million, but the credit will go elsewhere -- as usual. This morning's journal tells us something about the hookworm's operations:

The hookworm parasites often so lower the vitality of those who are affected as to retard their physical and mental development, render them more susceptible to other diseases, make labor less efficient, and in the sections where the malady is most prevalent greatly increase the death rate from consumption, pneumonia, typhoid fever and malaria. It has been shown that the lowered vitality of multitudes, long attributed to malaria and climate and seriously affecting economic development, is in fact due in some districts to this parasite. The disease is by no means confined to any one class; it takes its toll of suffering and death from the highly intelligent and well to do as well as from the less fortunate. It is a conservative estimate that two millions of our people are affected by this parasite. The disease is more common and more serious in children of school age than in other persons.

Widespread and serious as the infection is, there is still a most encouraging outlook. The disease can be easily recognized, readily and effectively treated and by simple and proper sanitary precautions successfully prevented [with God's help].

The poor children are under the Eye that never sleeps, you see. They have had that ill luck in all the ages. They and "the Lord's poor" -- as the sarcastic phrase goes -- have never been able to get away from that Eye's attentions.

Yes, the poor, the humble, the ignorant -- they are the ones that catch it. Take the "Sleeping Sickness," of Africa. This atrocious cruelty has for its victims a race of ignorant and unoffending blacks whom God placed in a remote wilderness, and bent his parental Eye upon them -- the one that never sleeps when there is a chance to breed sorrow for somebody. He arranged for these people before the Flood. The chosen agent was a fly, related to the tsetse; the tsetse is a fly which has command of the Zambezi country and stings cattle and horses to death, thus rendering that region uninhabitable by man. The tsetse's awful relative deposits a microbe which produces the Sleeping Sickness. Ham was full of these microbes, and when the voyage was over he discharged them in Africa and the havoc began, never to find amelioration until six thousand years should go by and science should pry into the mystery and hunt out the cause of the disease. The pious nations are now thanking God, and praising him for coming to the rescue of his poor blacks. The pulpit says the praise is due to him. He is surely a curious Being. He commits a fearful crime, continues that crime unbroken for six thousand years, and is then entitled to praise because he suggests to somebody else to modify its severities. He is called patient, and he certainly must be patient, or he would have sunk the pulpit in perdition ages ago for the ghastly compliments it pays him.

Science has this to say about the Sleeping Sickness, otherwise called the Negro Lethargy:

It is characterized by periods of sleep recurring at intervals. The disease lasts from four months to four years, and is always fatal. The victim appears at first languid, weak, pallid, and stupid. His eyelids become puffy, an eruption appears on his skin. He falls asleep while talking, eating, or working. As the disease progresses he is fed with difficulty and becomes much emaciated. The failure of nutrition and the appearance of bedsores are followed by convulsions and death. Some patients become insane.

It is he whom Church and people call Our Father in Heaven who has invented the fly and sent him to inflict this dreary long misery and melancholy and wretchedness, and decay of body and mind, upon a poor savage who has done that Great Criminal no harm. There isn't a man in the world who doesn't pity that poor black sufferer, and there isn't a man that wouldn't make him whole if he could. To find the one person who has no pity for him you must go to heaven; to find the one person who is able to heal him and couldn't be persuaded to do it, you must go to the same place. There is only one father cruel enough to afflict his child with that horrible disease -- only one. Not all the eternities can produce another one. Do you like reproachful poetical indignations warmly expressed? Here is one, hot from the heart of a slave:

Man's inhumanity to man
Makes countless thousands mourn!

I will tell you a pleasant tale which has in it a touch of pathos. A man got religion, and asked the priest what he must do to be worthy of his new estate. The priest said, "Imitate our Father in Heaven, learn to be like him." The man studied his Bible diligently and thoroughly and understandingly, and then with prayers for heavenly guidance instituted his imitations. He tricked his wife into falling downstairs, and she broke her back and became a paralytic for life; he betrayed his brother into the hands of a sharper, who robbed him of his all and landed him in the almshouse; he inoculated one son with hookworms, another with the sleeping sickness, another with gonorrhea; he furnished one daughter with scarlet fever and ushered her into her teens deaf, dumb, and blind for life; and after helping a rascal seduce the remaining one, he closed his doors against her and she died in a brothel cursing him. Then he reported to the priest, who said that *that* was no way to imitate his Father in Heaven. The convert asked wherein he had failed, but the priest changed the subject and inquired what kind of weather he was having, up his way.

Letter VIII

Man is without any doubt the most interesting fool there is. Also the most eccentric. He hasn't a single written law, in his Bible or out of it, which has any but just one purpose and intention -- to *limit or defeat the law of God*.

He can seldom take a plain fact and get any but a wrong meaning out of it. He cannot help this; it is the way the confusion he calls his mind is constructed. Consider the things he concedes, and the curious conclusions he draws from them.

For instance, he concedes that God made man. Made him without man's desire of privity.

This seems to plainly and indisputably make God, and God alone, responsible for man's acts. But man denies this.

He concedes that God has made the angels perfect, without blemish, and immune from pain and death, and that he could have been similarly kind to man if he had wanted to, but denies that he was under any moral obligation to do it.

He concedes that man has no moral right to visit the child of his begetting with wanton cruelties, painful diseases and death, but refuses to limit God's privileges in this sort with the children of his begetting.

The Bible and man's statutes forbid murder, adultery, fornication, lying, treachery, robbery, oppression and other crimes, but contend that God is free of these laws and has a right to break them when he will.

He concedes that God gives to each man his temperament, his disposition, at birth; he concedes that man cannot by any process change this temperament, but must remain always under its dominion. Yet if it be full of dreadful passions, in one man's case, and barren of them in another man's, it is right and rational to punish the one for his crimes, and reward the other for abstaining from crime.

There -- let us consider these curiosities.

Temperament (Disposition)

Take two extremes of temperament -- the goat and the tortoise.

Neither of these creatures makes its own temperament, but is born with it, like man, and can no more change it than can man.

Temperament is the law of God written in the heart of every creature by God's own hand, and *must* be obeyed, and will be obeyed in spite of all restricting or forbidding statutes, let them emanate whence they may.

Very well, lust is the dominant feature of the goat's temperament, the law of God is in its heart, and it must obey it and *will* obey it the whole day long in the rutting season, without stopping to eat or drink. If the Bible said to the goat, "Thou shalt not fornicate, thou shalt not commit adultery," even Man -- sap-headed man -- would recognize the foolishness of the prohibition, and would grant that the goat ought not to be punished for obeying the law of his Maker. Yet he thinks it right and just that man should be put under the prohibition. All men. All alike.

On its face this is stupid, for, by temperament, which is the *real law* of God, many men are goats and can't help committing adultery when they get a chance; whereas there are numbers of men who, by temperament, can keep their purity and let an opportunity go by if the woman lacks in attractiveness. But the Bible doesn't allow adultery at all, whether a person can help it or not. It allows no distinction between goat and tortoise -- the excitable goat, the emotional goat, that has to have some adultery every day or fade and die; and the tortoise, that cold calm puritan, that takes a treat only once in two years and then goes to sleep in the midst of it and doesn't wake up for sixty days. No lady goat is safe from criminal assault, even on the Sabbath Day, when there is a gentleman goat within three miles to leeward of her and nothing in the way but a fence fourteen feet high, whereas neither the gentleman tortoise nor the lady tortoise is ever hungry enough for solemn joys of fornication to be willing to break the Sabbath to get them. Now according to man's curious reasoning, the goat has earned punishment, and the tortoise praise.

"Thou shalt not commit adultery" is a command which makes no distinction between the following persons. They are all required to obey it:

Children at birth.
Children in the cradle.
School children.
Youths and maidens.
Fresh adults.
Older ones.
Men and women of 40.
Of 50.
Of 60.
Of 70.

Of 80.
Of 90.
Of 100.

The command does not distribute its burden equally, and cannot.

It is not hard upon the three sets of children.

It is hard -- harder -- still harder upon the next three sets -- cruelly hard.

It is blessedly softened to the next three sets.

It has now done all the damage it can, and might as well be put out of commission. Yet with comical imbecility it is continued, and the four remaining estates are put under its crushing ban. Poor old wrecks, they couldn't disobey if they tried. And think -- because they holily refrain from adulterating each other, they get praise for it! Which is nonsense; for even the Bible knows enough to know that if the oldest veteran there could get his lost heyday back again for an hour he would cast that commandment to the winds and ruin the first woman he came across, even though she were an entire stranger.

It is as I have said: every statute in the Bible and in the law-books is an attempt to defeat a law of God -- in other words an unalterable and indestructible law of nature. These people's God has shown them by a million acts that he respects none of the Bible's statutes. He breaks every one of the himself, adultery and all.

The law of God, as quite plainly expressed in woman's construction is this: There shall be no limit put upon your intercourse with the other sex sexually, at any time of life.

The law of God, as quite plainly expressed in man's construction is this: During your entire life you shall be under inflexible limits and restrictions, sexually.

During twenty-three days in every month (in absence of pregnancy) from the time a woman is seven years old till she dies of old age, she is ready for action, and *competent*. As competent as the candlestick is to receive the candle. Competent every day, competent every night. Also she *wants* that candle -- yearns for it, longs for it, hankers after it, as commanded by the law of God in her heart.

But man is only briefly competent; and only then in the moderate measure applicable to the word in *his* sex's case. He is competent from the age of sixteen or seventeen thence-forward for thirty-five years. After fifty his performance is of poor quality, the intervals between are wide, and its satisfactions of no great value to either party; whereas his great-grandmother is as good as new. There is nothing the matter with her plant. Her candlestick is as firm as ever, whereas his candle is increasingly softened and weakened by the weather of age, as the years go by, until at last it can no longer stand, and is mournfully laid to rest in the hope of a blessed resurrection which is never to come.

By the woman's make, her plant has to be out of service three days in the month, and during a part of her pregnancy. These are times of discomfort, often of suffering. For fair and just compensation she has the high privilege of unlimited adultery all the other days of her life.

That is the law of God, as revealed in her make. What becomes of this high privilege? Does she live in free enjoyment of it? No. Nowhere in the whole world. She is robbed of it everywhere. Who does this? Man. Man's statutes -- if the Bible *is* the Word of God.

Now there you have a sample of man's "reasoning powers," as he calls them. He observes certain facts. For instance, that in all his life he never sees the day that he can satisfy one woman; also, that no woman ever sees the day that she can't overwork, and defeat, and put out of commission any ten masculine plants that can be put to bed to her.[2] He puts those strikingly suggestive and luminous facts together, and from them draws this astonishing conclusion: The Creator intended the woman to be restricted to one man.

So he concretes that singular conclusion into *law*, for good and all.

And he does it without consulting the woman, although she has a thousand times more at stake in the matter than he has. His procreative competency is limited to an average of a hundred exercises per year for fifty years, hers is good for three thousand a year for that whole time -- and as many years longer as she may live. Thus his life interest in the matter is five thousand refreshments, while hers is a hundred and fifty thousand; yet instead of fairly and honorably leaving the making of the law to the person who has an overwhelming interest at stake in it, this immeasurable hog, who has nothing at stake in it worth considering, makes it himself!

You have heretofore found out, by my teachings, that man is a fool; you are now aware that woman is a damned fool.

---

[2]   In the Sandwich Islands in 1866 a buxom royal princess died. Occupying a place of distinguished honor at her funeral were thirty-six splendidly built young native men. In a laudatory song which celebrated the various merits, achievements and accomplishments of the late princess those thirty-six stallions were called her *harem*, and the song said it had been her pride and boast that she kept the whole of them busy, and that several times it had happened that more than one of them had been able to charge overtime. [M.T.]

Now if you or any other really intelligent person were arranging the fairness and justices between man and woman, you would give the man one-fiftieth interest in one woman, and the woman a harem. Now wouldn't you? Necessarily. I give you my word, this creature with the decrepit candle has arranged it exactly the other way. Solomon, who was one of the Deity's favorites, had a copulation cabinet composed of seven hundred wives and three hundred concubines. To save his life he could not have kept two of these young creatures satisfactorily refreshed, even if he had had fifteen experts to help him. Necessarily almost the entire thousand had to go hungry years and years on a stretch. Conceive of a man hardhearted enough to look daily upon all that suffering and not be moved to mitigate it. He even wantonly added a sharp pang to that pathetic misery; for he kept within those women's sight, always, stalwart watchmen whose splendid masculine forms made the poor lassies' mouths water but who hadn't anything to solace a candlestick with, these gentry being eunuchs. A eunuch is a person whose candle has been put out. By art.[3]

From time to time, as I go along, I will take up a Biblical statute and show you that it always violates a law of God, and then is imported into the lawbooks of the nations, where it continues its violations. But those things will keep; there is no hurry.

---

[3] I purpose publishing these Letters here in the world before I return to you. Two editions. One, unedited, for Bible readers and their children; the other, expurgated, for persons of refinement. [M.T.]

Letter IX

The Ark continued its voyage, drifting around here and there and yonder, compassless and uncontrolled, the sport of the random winds and swirling currents. And the rain, the rain, the rain! It kept falling, pouring, drenching, flooding. No such rain had ever been seen before. Sixteen inches a day had been heard of, but that was nothing to this. This was a hundred and twenty inches a day -- ten feet! At this incredible rate it rained forty days and forty nights, and submerged every hill that was four hundred feet high. Then the heavens and even the angels went dry; no more water was to be had.

As a Universal flood it was a disappointment, but there had been heaps of Universal Floods before, as is witnessed by all the Bibles of all the nations, and this was as good as the best one.

At last the Ark soared aloft and came to rest on top of Mount Ararat, seventeen thousand feet above the valley, and its living freight got out and went down the mountain.

Noah planted a vineyard, and drank the wine and was overcome.

This person had been selected from all the populations because he was the best sample there was. He was to start the human race on a new basis. This was the new basis. The promise was bad. To go further with the experiment was to run a great and most unwise risk. Now was the time to do with these people what had been so judiciously done with the others -- drown them. Anybody but the Creator would have seen this. But he didn't see it. That is, maybe he didn't.

It is claimed that from the beginning of time he foresaw everything that would happen in the world. If that is true, he foresaw that Adam and Eve would eat the apple; that their posterity would be unendurable and have to be drowned; that Noah's posterity would in their turn be unendurable, and that by and by he would have to leave his throne in heaven and come down and be crucified to save that same tiresome human race again. The whole of it? No! A part of it? Yes. Now much of it? In each generation, for hundreds and hundreds of generations, a billion would die and all go to perdition except perhaps ten thousand out of the billion. The ten thousand would have to come from the little body of Christians, and only one in the hundred of that little body would stand any chance. None of them at all except such Roman Catholics as should have the luck to have a priest handy to sandpaper their souls at the last gasp, and here and there a presbyterian. No others savable. All the others damned. By the million.

Shall you grant that he foresaw all this? The pulpit grants it. It is the same as granting that in the matter of intellect the Deity is the Head Pauper of the Universe, and that in the matter of morals and character he is away down on the level of David.

Letter X

The two Testaments are interesting, each in its own way. The Old one gives us a picture of these people's Deity as he was before he got religion, the other one gives us a picture of him as he appeared afterward. The Old Testament is interested mainly in blood and sensuality. The New one in Salvation. Salvation by fire.

The first time the Deity came down to earth, he brought life and death; when he came the second time, he brought hell.

Life was not a valuable gift, but death was. Life was a fever-dream made up of joys embittered by sorrows, pleasure poisoned by pain, a dream that was a nightmare-confusion of spasmodic and fleeting delights, ecstasies, exultations, happinesses, interspersed with long-drawn miseries, griefs, perils, horrors, disappointments, defeats, humiliations, and despairs -- the heaviest curse devisable by divine ingenuity; but death was sweet, death was gentle, death was kind; death healed the bruised spirit and the broken heart, and gave them rest and forgetfulness; death was man's best friend; when man could endure life no longer, death came and set him free.

In time, the Deity perceived that death was a mistake; a mistake, in that it was insufficient; insufficient, for the reason that while it was an admirable agent for the inflicting of misery upon the survivor, it allowed the dead person himself to escape from all further persecution in the blessed refuge of the grave. This was not satisfactory. A way must be conceived to pursue the dead beyond the tomb.

The Deity pondered this matter during four thousand years unsuccessfully, but as soon as he came down to earth and became a Christian his mind cleared and he knew what to do. He invented hell, and proclaimed it.

Now here is a curious thing. It is believed by everybody that while he was in heaven he was stern, hard, resentful, jealous, and cruel; but that when he came down to earth and assumed the name Jesus Christ, he became the opposite of what he was before: that is to say, he became sweet, and gentle, merciful, forgiving, and all harshness disappeared from his nature and a deep and yearning love for his poor human children took its place. Whereas it was as Jesus Christ that he devised hell and proclaimed it!

Which is to say, that as the meek and gentle Savior he was a thousand billion times crueler than ever he was in the Old Testament -- oh, incomparably more atrocious than ever he was when he was at the very worst in those old days!

Meek and gentle? By and by we will examine this popular sarcasm by the light of the hell which he invented.

While it is true that the palm for malignity must be granted to Jesus, the inventor of hell, he was hard and ungentle enough for all godlike purposes even before he became a Christian. It does not appear that he ever stopped to reflect that *he* was to blame when a man went wrong, inasmuch as the man was merely acting in accordance with the disposition he had afflicted him with. No, he punished the man, instead of punishing himself. Moreover, the punishment usually oversized the offense. Often, too, it fell, not upon the doer of a misdeed, but upon somebody else -- a chief man, the head of a community, for instance.

And Israel abode in Shittim, and the people began to commit whoredom with the daughters of Moab.

And the Lord said unto Moses, Take all the heads of the people, and hang them up before the Lord against the Sun, that the fierce anger of the Lord may be turned away from Israel.

Does that look fair to you? It does not appear that the "heads of the people" got any of the adultery, yet it is they that are hanged, instead of "the people."

If it was fair and right in that day it would be fair and right today, for the pulpit maintains that God's justice is eternal and unchangeable; also that he is the Fountain of Morals, and that his morals are eternal and unchangeable. Very well, then, we must believe that if the people of New York should begin to commit whoredom with the daughters of New Jersey, it would be fair and right to set up a gallows in front of the city hall and hang the mayor and the sheriff and the judges and the archbishop on it, although they did not get any of it. It does not look right to me.

Moreover, you may be quite sure of one thing: it couldn't happen. These people would not allow it. They are better than their Bible. *Nothing* would happen here, except some lawsuits, for damages, if the incident couldn't be hushed up; and even down South they would not proceed against persons who did not get any of it; they would get a rope and hunt for the correspondents, and if they couldn't find them they would lynch a nigger.

Things have greatly improved since the Almighty's time, let the pulpit say what it may.

Will you examine the Deity's morals and disposition and conduct a little further? And will you remember that in the Sunday school the little children are urged to love the Almighty, and honor him, and praise him, and make him their model and try to be as like him as they can? Read:

1 And the Lord spake unto Moses, saying,

2 Avenge the children of Israel of the Midianites: afterward shalt thou be gathered unto thy people....

7 And they warred against the Midianites, as the Lord commanded Moses; and they slew all the males.

8 And they slew the kings of Midian, beside the rest of them that were slain; *namely*, Evi, and Rekem, and Zur, and Hur, and Reba, five kings of Midian: Balaam also the son of Beor they slew with the sword.

9 And the children of Israel took *all* the women of Midian captives, and their little ones, and took the spoil of all their cattle, and all their flocks, and all their goods.

10 And they burnt all their cities wherein they dwelt, and all their goodly castles, with fire.

11 And they took all the spoil, and all the prey, *both* of men and of beasts.

12 And they brought the captives, and the prey, and the spoil unto Moses, and Eleazar the priest, and unto the congregation of the children of Israel, unto the camp at the plains of Moab, which *are* by Jordan *near* Jericho.

13 And Moses, and Eleazar the priest, and all the princes of the congregation, went forth to meet them without the camp.

14 And Moses was wroth with the officers of the host, *with* the captains over thousands, and captains over hundreds, which came from the battle.

15 And Moses said unto them, Have ye saved all the women alive?

16 Behold, these caused the children of Israel, through the counsel of Balaam, to commit trespass against the Lord in the matter of Peor, and there was a plague among the congregation of the Lord.

17 Now therefore kill every male among the little ones, and kill every woman that hath known man by lying with him.

18 But all the women children, that have not known a man by lying with him, keep alive for yourselves.

19 And do ye abide without the camp seven days: whosoever hath killed any person, and whosoever hath touched any slain, purify *both* yourselves and your captives on the third day, and on the seventh day.

20 And purify all *your* raiment, and all that is made of skins, and all work of goats' *hair*, and all things made of wood.

21 And Eleazar the priest said unto the men of war which went to the battle, This *is* the ordinance of the law which the Lord commanded Moses....

25 And the Lord spake unto Moses, saying,

26 Take the sum of the prey that was taken, both of man and of beast, thou, and Eleazar the priest, and the chief fathers of the congregation:

27 And divide the prey into two parts; between them that took the war upon them, who went out to battle, and between all the congregation:

28 And levy a tribute unto the Lord of the men of war which went out to battle....

31 And Moses and Eleazar the priest did as the Lord commanded Moses.

32 And the booty, *being* the rest of the prey which the men of war had caught, was six hundred thousand and seventy thousand and five thousand sheep,

33 And threescore and twelve thousand beeves,

34 And threescore and one thousand asses,

35 And thirty and two thousand persons in all, of woman that had not known man by lying with him....

40 And the persons *were* sixteen thousand; of which the Lord's tribute *was* thirty and two persons.

41 And Moses gave the tribute, *which* was the Lord's heave offering, unto Eleazar the priest, as the Lord commanded Moses....

47 Even of the children of Israel's half, Moses took one portion of fifty, *both* of man and of beast, and gave them unto the Levites, which kept the charge of the tabernacle of the Lord; as the Lord commanded Moses.

10 When thou comest nigh unto a city to fight against it, then proclaim peace unto it....

13 And when the Lord thy God hath delivered it into thine hands, thou shalt smite every male thereof with the edge of the sword:

14 But the women, and the little ones, and the cattle, and all that is in the city, *even* all the spoil thereof, shalt thou take unto thyself; and thou shalt eat the spoil of thine enemies, which the Lord thy God hath given thee.

15 Thus shalt thou do unto all the cities *which* are very far off from thee, which are not of the cities of these nations.

16 But of the cities of these people, which the Lord thy God doth give thee for an inheritance, thou shalt save alive nothing that breatheth:

The Biblical law says: "Thou shalt not kill."

The law of God, planted in the heart of man at his birth, says: "Thou shalt kill."

The chapter I have quoted shows you that the book-statute is once more a failure. It cannot set aside the more powerful law of nature.

According to the belief of these people, it was God himself who said: "Thou shalt not kill."

Then it is plain that he cannot keep his own commandments.

He killed all those people -- every male.

They had offended the Deity in some way. We know what the offense was, without looking; that is to say, we know it was a trifle; some small thing that no one but a god would attach any importance to. It is more than likely that a Midianite had been duplicating the conduct of one Onan, who was commanded to "go into his brother's wife" -- which he did; but instead of finishing, "he spilled it on the ground." The Lord slew Onan for that, for the lord could never abide indelicacy. The Lord slew Onan, and to this day the Christian world cannot understand why he stopped with Onan, instead of slaying all the inhabitants for three hundred miles around -- they being innocent of offense, and therefore the very ones he would usually slay. For that had always been his idea of fair dealing. If he had had a motto, it would have read, "Let no innocent person escape." You remember what he did in the time of the flood. There were multitudes and multitudes of tiny little children, and he knew they had never done him any harm; but their relations had, and that was enough for him: he saw the waters rise toward their screaming lips, he saw the wild terror in their eyes, he saw that agony of appeal in the mothers' faces which would have touched any heart but

55

his, but he was after the guiltless particularly, than he drowned those poor little chaps.

And you will remember that in the case of Adam's posterity *all* the billions are innocent -- none of them had a share in his offense, but the Deity holds them guilty to this day. None gets off, except by acknowledging that guilt -- no cheaper lie will answer.

Some Midianite must have repeated Onan's act, and brought that dire disaster upon his nation. If that was not the indelicacy that outraged the feelings of the Deity, then I know what it was: some Midianite had been pissing against the wall. I am sure of it, for that was an impropriety which the Source of all Etiquette never could stand. A person could piss against a tree, he could piss on his mother, he could piss on his own breeches, and get off, but he must not piss against the wall -- that would be going quite too far. The origin of the divine prejudice against this humble crime is not stated; but we know that the prejudice was very strong -- so strong that nothing but a wholesale massacre of the people inhabiting the region where the wall was defiled could satisfy the Deity.

Take the case of Jeroboam. "I will cut off from Jeroboam him that pisseth against the wall." It was done. And not only was the man that did it cut off, but everybody else.

The same with the house of Baasha: everybody was exterminated, kinsfolks, friends, and all, leaving "not one that pisseth against a wall."

In the case of Jeroboam you have a striking instance of the Deity's custom of not limiting his punishments to the guilty; the innocent are included. Even the "remnant" of that unhappy house was removed, even "as a man taketh away dung, till it be all gone." That includes the women, the young maids, and the little girls. All innocent, for they couldn't piss against a wall. Nobody of that sex can. None but members of the other sex can achieve that feat.

A curious prejudice. And it still exists. Protestant parents still keep the Bible handy in the house, so that the children can study it, and one of the first things the little boys and girls learn is to be righteous and holy and not piss against the wall. They study those passages more than they study any others, except those which incite to masturbation. Those they hunt out and study in private. No Protestant child exists who does not masturbate. That art is the earliest accomplishment his religion confers upon him. Also the earliest her religion confers upon her.

The Bible has this advantage over all other books that teach refinement and good manners: that it goes to the child. It goes to the mind at its most impressible and receptive age -- the others have to wait.

"Thou shalt have a paddle upon thy weapon; and it shall be, when thou wilt ease thyself abroad, thou shalt dig therewith, and shalt turn back and cover that which cometh from thee."

That rule was made in the old days because "The Lord thy God walketh in the midst of thy camp."

It is probably not worthwhile to try to find out, for certain, why the Midianites were exterminated. We can only be sure that it was for no large offense; for the cases of Adam, and the Flood, and the defilers of the wall teach us that much. A Midianite may have left his paddle at home and thus brought on the trouble. However, it is no matter. The main thing is the trouble itself, and the morals of one kind and another that it offers for the instruction and elevation of the Christian of today.

God wrote upon the tables of stone: "Thou shalt not kill," Also: "Thou shalt not commit adultery."

Paul, speaking by the divine voice, advised against sexual intercourse *altogether*. A great change from the divine view as it existed at the time of the Midianite incident.

Letter XI

Human history in all ages is red with blood, and bitter with hate, and stained with cruelties; but not since Biblical times have these features been without a limit of some kind. Even the Church, which is credited with having spilt more innocent blood, since the beginning of its supremacy, than all the political wars put together have spilt, has observed a limit. A sort of limit. But you notice that when the Lord God of Heaven and Earth, adored Father of Man, goes to war, there is no limit. He is totally without mercy -- he, who is called the Fountain of Mercy. He slays, slays, slays! All the men, all the beasts, all the boys, all the babies; also all the women and all the girls, except those that have not been deflowered.

He makes no distinction between innocent and guilty. The babies were innocent, the beasts were innocent, many of the men, many of the women, many of the boys, many of the girls were innocent, yet they had to suffer with the guilty. What the insane Father required was blood and misery; he was indifferent as to who furnished it.

The heaviest punishment of all was meted out to persons who could not by any possibility have deserved so horrible a fate -- the 32,000 virgins. Their naked privacies were probed, to make sure that they still possessed the hymen unruptured; after this humiliation they were sent away from the land that had been their home, to be sold into slavery; the worst of slaveries and the shamefulest, the slavery of prostitution; bed-slavery, to excite lust, and satisfy it with their bodies; slavery to any buyer, be he gentleman or be he a coarse and filthy ruffian.

It was the Father that inflicted this ferocious and undeserved punishment upon those bereaved and friendless virgins, whose parents and kindred he had slaughtered before their eyes. And were they praying to him for pity and rescue, meantime? Without a doubt of it.

These virgins were "spoil" plunder, booty. He claimed his share and got it. What use had *he* for virgins? Examine his later history and you will know.

His priests got a share of the virgins, too. What use could priests make of virgins? The private history of the Roman Catholic confessional can answer that question for you. The confessional's chief amusement has been seduction -- in all the ages of the Church. Père Hyacinth testifies that of a hundred priests confessed by him, ninety-nine had used the confessional effectively for the seduction of married women and young girls. One priest confessed that of nine hundred girls and women whom he had served as father and confessor in his time, none had escaped his lecherous embrace but he elderly and the homely. The official list of questions which the priest is required to ask will overmasteringly excite any woman who is not a paralytic.

There is nothing in either savage or civilized history that is more utterly complete, more remorselessly sweeping than the Father of Mercy's campaign among the Midianites. The official report does not furnish the incidents, episodes, and minor details, it deals only in information in masses: *all* the virgins, *all* the men, *all* the babies, *all* "creatures *that breathe*," *all* houses, *all* cities; it gives you just one vast picture, spread abroad here and there and yonder, as far as eye can reach, of charred ruin and storm-swept desolation; your imagination adds a brooding stillness, an awful hush -- the hush of death. But of course there were incidents. Where shall we get them?

Out of history of yesterday's date. Out of history made by the red Indian of America. He has duplicated God's work, and done it in the very spirit of God. In 1862 the Indians in Minnesota, having been deeply wronged and treacherously treated by the government of the United States, rose against the white settlers and massacred them; massacred all they could lay their hands upon, sparing neither age nor sex. Consider this incident:

Twelve Indians broke into a farmhouse at daybreak and captured the family. It consisted of the farmer and his wife and four daughters, the youngest aged fourteen and the eldest eighteen. They crucified the parents; that is to say, they stood them stark naked against the wall of the living room and nailed their hands to the wall. Then they stripped the daughters bare, stretched them upon the floor in front of their parents, and repeatedly ravished them. Finally they crucified the girls against the wall opposite this parents, and cut off their noses and their breasts. They also -- but I will not go into that. There is a limit. There are indignities so atrocious that the pen cannot write them. One member of that poor crucified family -- the father -- was still alive when help came two days later.

Now you have one incident of the Minnesota massacre. I could give you fifty. They would cover all the different kinds of cruelty the brutal human talent has ever invented.

And now you know, by these sure indications, what happened under the personal direction of the Father of Mercies in his Midianite campaign. The Minnesota campaign was merely a duplicate of the Midianite raid. Nothing happened in the one that didn't happen in the other.

No, that is not strictly true. The Indian was more merciful than was the Father of Mercies. He sold no virgins into slavery to minister to the lusts of the murderers of their kindred while their sad lives might last;

he raped them, then charitably made their subsequent sufferings brief, ending them with the precious gift of death. He burned some of the houses, but not all of them. He carried out innocent dumb brutes, but he took the lives of none.

Would you expect this same conscienceless God, this moral bankrupt, to become a teacher of morals; of gentleness; of meekness; of righteousness; of purity? It looks impossible, extravagant; but listen to him. These are his own words:

Blessed are the poor in spirit, for theirs is the kingdom of heaven.

Blessed are they that mourn, for they shall be comforted.

Blessed are the meek, for they shall inherit the earth.

Blessed are they which do hunger and thirst after righteousness, for they shall be filled.

Blessed are the merciful, for they shall obtain mercy.

Blessed are the pure in heart, for they shall see God.

Blessed are the peacemakers, for they shall be called the children of God.

Blessed are they which are persecuted for righteousness' sake, for theirs is the kingdom of heaven.

Blessed are ye, when men shall revile you, and persecute you, and say all manner of evil against you falsely, for my sake.

The mouth that uttered these immense sarcasms, these giant hypocrisies, is the very same that ordered the wholesale massacre of the Midianitish men and babies and cattle; the wholesale destruction of house and city; the wholesale banishment of the virgins into a filthy and unspeakable slavery. This is the same person who brought upon the Midianites the fiendish cruelties which were repeated by the red Indians, detail by detail, in Minnesota eighteen centuries later. The Midianite episode filled him with joy. So did the Minnesota one, or he would have prevented it.

The Beatitudes and the quoted chapters from Numbers and Deuteronomy ought always to be read from the pulpit together; then the congregation would get an all-round view of Our Father in Heaven. Yet not in a single instance have I ever known a clergyman to do this.